Hubert
and the
Moon

Hubert
and the
Moon

Catherine Knight

Matador
9 Priory Business Park,
Wistow Road, Kibworth Beauchamp,
Leicestershire. LE8 0RX
Tel: (+44) 116 279 2299
Fax: (+44) 116 279 2277
Email: books@troubador.co.uk
Web: www.troubador.co.uk/matador

ISBN 978 1783065 301

British Library Cataloguing in Publication Data.
A catalogue record for this book is available from the British Library.

Typeset by Troubador Publishing Ltd, Leicester, UK
Printed and bound by CPI Group (UK) Ltd, Croydon, CR0 4YY

Matador is an imprint of Troubador Publishing Ltd

For Alice

CONTENTS

INTRODUCTION

A long time ago, when the world was a very different place, there lived a hare called Hubert who had a strange meeting with the moon. This was the beginning of a long adventure for Hubert and his friends, Petronella and Benedict. Join the three travellers to find out where they go and who they meet on the way. They will cross paths with a pirate, run into a retinue of rats, get lost in a crowd of children, get rescued by a saint and have an encounter with a crocodile. Will they all get safely home again? Oh, and look out for Old Mag – she is trouble!

CHAPTER 1

THE HARE

The year was twelve hundred and twelve. It was an age of magic, mystery and superstition.

England was ruled by King John, who was really rather grumpy and quarrelsome. He had been to Ireland and quarrelled with the Irish lords. Then, he came back to England and quarrelled with the English barons, and now, he was in France, quarrelling with the French king.

Hubert sat in a hollow between thickets of gorse and briar. He didn't know what year it was, he didn't know about King John, in fact he didn't know very much at all. Hubert was a hare.

Hubert shuffled around in his hollow and glanced across at his mother, who was sitting nearby. She sat very still, listening with her tall black tipped ears and looking with bright amber eyes.

"Soon you will be old enough to explore the meadow on your own," Hubert's mother said. "But you must take care; beware of the cat, the dog and the dragon. If you lie still, they may not see you. If they see you, you must run swiftly."

Hubert's eyes widened. "What is a cat, a dog and a dragon?" he asked.

"A cat," his mother said, "is silent as she stalks her prey. She leaps with dagger-like claws outstretched: she may surprise you. A dog is noisy and rough: he may frighten you. A dragon," she paused, "well, you will know if you see one."

Hubert's eyes narrowed a little.

"I know there are many things you do not understand," she said, "but I don't know all the answers myself. If you want to

1

know more about this strange, beautiful but dangerous world, you will have to ask Benedict."

"Who's Benedict?" asked Hubert.

His mother sighed. *Not another question!*

"Benedict is a very old hare," his mother replied. "He lives at the far side of the meadow between the tall silver birch tree and the edge of the stream."

Hubert gazed dreamily across the meadow towards the silver birch, whose leaves were beginning to turn yellow, and shivered in the cool breeze.

On the top-most branch of the silver birch tree sat Old Mag. She had blue-black feathers down her back, that looked like a shabby cloak, and white feathers on her front, that looked like a ragged apron. She watched Hubert with one eye, in fact, she only had one eye. Maybe she fancied something small and furry for her dinner. Hubert looked at Old Mag and was just about to ask about this strange one-eyed creature, when he noticed that his mother was already making her way through the tall grass towards the stream.

Cautiously, he looked all around, he listened, and then he took a giant and undignified leap. He had often seen his mother leap from her hollow to make it more difficult for enemies to follow her scent, and Hubert was sure that there were enemies hiding in the undergrowth or lurking in the trees. After several more leaps in several different directions, he bounded across the meadow towards the tall silver birch tree. He was so busy trying to look all around him that he didn't really look where he was going. Just before he reached the hedgerow he collided with something warm, furry and rather cross.

"Mother!" he cried. But it wasn't his mother – this creature was smaller and had much shorter ears, a much longer tail and stripes!

"Are… are you a dragon?" he asked. Hubert had never seen a cat before.

"There's no such thing as a dragon," came the reply. "I'm a kitten. My name is Petronella and soon I will be a cat."

Hubert hoped that Petronella would not change into a cat too soon as he remembered his mother's warning.

"Do you live in the meadow?" asked Hubert shyly.

"Certainly not", said Petronella. "I live with my mother and three brothers over there, in the cottage."

Hubert looked beyond the hedge and row of trees, and, in the distance, he could see a cottage roof from which curls of grey smoke appeared and then disappeared into the ever-darkening sky. Hubert shivered. The air was cool and damp for an early autumn evening, but it was not the weather that caused Hubert's discomfort, it was the thought of such a large quantity of cats!

"Don't worry," she said, "I won't let my brothers bully you. We shall be friends."

Hubert was a little comforted by this, he needed a friend and he hoped that Petronella would defend him as she had so confidently promised. They walked together through the tussocks of damp grass. A couple of bees droned past their ears, complaining about the dreary, dismal weather.

CHAPTER 2

THE CATS

The cottage where Petronella lived was low and dark. There was no chimney; the smoke from the fire puffed up through the room and escaped through a small window-like opening, near to the roof. There were two rooms; one was a bedroom and the other was where the lady of the house spent her day, preparing food and taking care of her animals. The lady of the house was Dame Grizel. She was very old and had lived in the tiny cottage for many years.

On this particular day, Dame Grizel was pottering in her back yard. It had rained heavily that day, and the pea-plants and beanstalks dripped and drooped towards the muddy earth below. The wind had blown fiercely and had tried to uproot the little vegetable plot. Most of the apples and plums had been knocked from their branches by the stormy weather, and the old lady stooped to rescue the bruised fruit.

Hiding amongst the peas and beans was Bartholomew. Bartholomew was a large, brown, tabby cat and he took great delight in jumping out of the undergrowth and startling poor Dame Grizel.

"Bless me! Barty, what a bad cat! You're soaked through – and look at those muddy paws. Where are your brothers?" she asked, as she stroked Bartholomew's damp fur.

There was a rustling among the leeks and the cabbages, and out on to the path leapt Maurice, closely followed by Mortimer. Mortimer was a dark tabby, like his brother Bartholomew, but Maurice was as black as the night.

Bartholomew playfully tapped Maurice's tail with his paw.

Maurice turned and cuffed Bartholomew's ear, then leapt on to a low branch of the apple tree. The two tabby cats chased Maurice, but were distracted from their game by a pair of wasps. The wasps had found the last remaining apple on the tree. Bartholomew flicked his bushy tail and wondered whether or not to annoy the wasps. He decided he couldn't be bothered.

"Why don't you three naughty boys do something useful like catching a few rats?" suggested Dame Grizel.

Mortimer stretched, Maurice yawned and Bartholomew mewed some excuse about feeling tired. The three of them trotted into the cottage, leaving a trail of muddy paw prints, as they made their way towards the hearth where their mother was already curled up asleep.

"I wonder where Petronella has got to," Dame Grizel said to herself, "I hope she is safe."

The Dame knew that some of the villagers disliked her cats. She worried if they were away from home for too long, and it was getting quite dark. She went inside, but left the door ajar, as she was expecting Petronella to return quite soon. It was very gloomy inside, so the old woman took a rush-light over to the fire, lit one end, then placed the flickering flame in the centre of her trestle table. Three chickens, disturbed by the light, fidgeted in the corner of the room before settling back down to roost.

A metal pot hung over the fire and inside was some soup she had made from the vegetables picked from her garden. She was just about to serve herself some soup when two of her cats suddenly sat up, their ears twitching. In the distance she could hear footsteps. The footsteps grew louder and there was the sound of angry voices.

The other cats jumped to their feet: Bartholomew arched his back, Mortimer made a low growling noise and Maurice shrank back into the shadows so that all you could see were his eyes glinting in the firelight.

Dame Grizel reached towards the door but it was too late; the door swung open and in marched four large and unwelcome visitors. The Dame recognised the leader of the group. It was the miller: a big, brawny fellow who usually meant trouble. He had an untidy beard – red like a fox – and on the end of his broad nose was a wart. His companions were peasant farmers from the village. The miller raised his hand and pointed at Dame Grizel.

"We know about your mischief old witch," he shouted, "you and your cats, your cauldron and your black magic!"

"I don't know what you mean," said the old woman in a timid voice. "There's no magic potion in my pot – it's vegetable soup!"

"I blame those evil cats," declared one of the farmers. "They've brought a curse on this land. Most of the crops which we have grown have been washed away by rain and storms. The wind has damaged our barns and our grain will rot. The cats must go."

Meanwhile, Petronella and Hubert had arrived outside the cottage and were startled to hear the commotion going on inside. There was a great deal of hissing and spitting, clucking of chickens, shouting, weeping and clattering of furniture.

"Quickly," whispered Petronella to Hubert, "behind this pile of old wood."

The kitten and the hare hid among the logs and branches that the Dame had collected for firewood. They watched in horror as the brutish miller and his heartless companions carried away Petronella's family. Old Mag sat on the roof and also watched.

"Good," she said to herself, glancing at the frightened chickens and thinking about stealing some tasty fresh eggs.

At first, Petronella and Hubert were too terrified to move, but when the men were out of sight, they cautiously emerged from their hiding place and crept through the open doorway. Dame Grizel sat at the table, her head in her hands. Her discarded supper had gone cold and the fire had almost gone out. Petronella mewed.

"Petronella," murmured the Dame, "is that you?"

With tearful eyes she peered through the gloom and could just recognise the shape of her youngest cat. She re-lit the rush-light that had gone out in the scuffle with the farmers. She turned, and was surprised to see that Petronella was not alone.

"Who have you brought home with you?" asked the Dame. "Is it a rabbit?" She looked closer and noticed Hubert's long ears tipped with black, his long legs and angular little face. "Well I never," she cried, "it's a hare!" Suddenly her expression changed from one of delight to one of anxiety.

"Petronella, you cannot stay here," she said. "The miller has taken away your mother and brothers. He has blamed us for the bad weather and will only allow the cats to return if I make sure that the sun shines on their land. I cannot alter the weather, I know of no magic that will save their harvest, I don't know what to do."

Fresh tears began to flow down the old woman's cheeks as she said farewell to her last little cat. Petronella turned and went slowly back through the open door into the night, Hubert at her side. For the first time since Hubert had met Petronella, she was silent. He knew that he must think of some way to help his young companion. He thought of his mother. She said that a cat may surprise him, she was right. He tried to remember what else she had said.

Benedict, he thought, *that's it, Benedict, he will know what to do*.

Chapter 3

The Moon

Petronella trotted out of the garden and into the meadow. Hubert scampered after her.

"Wait for me," he called. Petronella looked over her shoulder. "Listen Petronella, this problem is too difficult for us to work out, we must find help. There's an old hare called Benedict who lives over by the stream, we will ask him what we should do." Petronella looked unconvinced,

"Hares don't usually have much to do with cats," she said.

"Cats don't usually have much to do with hares," replied Hubert. "But you wanted to be my friend."

Petronella reluctantly agreed, and Hubert led the way through the undergrowth. The moon appeared from behind the clouds. Her silvery beams painted the bark of the birch tree white and glittered on the black water of the nearby stream. Just beyond the tree, almost hidden beneath a canopy of wild honeysuckle, were the remains of an old wooden cart. One wheel had been placed on the ground and, in-between the spokes, grew a variety of plants. Hubert sniffed the little cartwheel garden.

"Be careful," warned a voice from the darkness. "Some of those herbs are for medicines only."

From beneath the upturned cart, the owner of the voice shuffled towards his unexpected visitors. As he appeared from the shadows into the moonlight, Petronella and Hubert were able to see the large elderly hare. His fur was tinged with grey, his white whiskers shone like silver, and his back was a little bent over.

"Well, well," exclaimed Benedict, "it's a little late for you two young creatures to be out on your own."

"Please sir," began Hubert nervously, "I want to help my new friend Petronella, but it is too dangerous for her to go home because the farmers have stolen her family and Dame Grizel cannot make the sun shine and…"

"Please stop," interrupted Benedict, clasping his paws together. "I think you should both come inside and explain what has happened… slowly!"

Benedict turned, and led them through a doorway. Inside it was warm and dry with sweet smelling herbs strewn on the floor. The three animals made themselves comfortable, and Petronella and Hubert told Benedict everything that had happened that day. There was a long silence while Benedict considered their story. Hubert fidgeted nervously and Petronella washed her face, twice. At last the wise old hare suddenly looked inspired.

"Sleep is the answer," he said.

Hubert and Petronella looked at each other, then looked

back to Benedict. Benedict was amused at their puzzled expressions and explained further. "Complicated problems are always impossible to solve at night. Bedtime is not the time for worry, bedtime is for sleeping. The dawn will bring new light to this question, and then we will be able to see the answer." Petronella began to protest, but suddenly noticed how tired she was and said that maybe Benedict was right.

They settled down for the night. They could hear rustlings in the meadow as the night creatures went about their business. A hungry fox searched the hedgerow for food, but was unaware of the inhabitants of the old cart house.

Hubert didn't sleep very well. The events of the day kept going round and round in his mind. His long ears picked up every sound from outside, and the moon shone through a crack in the roof, lighting up the unfamiliar surroundings. He looked over at his new friends; both were fast asleep. He decided to stretch his long legs and made his way quietly to the door.

Hubert peered out into the meadow. Everywhere was silent. The rain clouds had drifted away and the moon shone with a strange, magical light. Hubert glanced up into the sky and thought that the moon appeared to have a face. He looked again, longer this time, and to his astonishment the moon began to change shape. It grew longer and thinner and the face became clearer. Hubert's eyes grew wide with wonder as the moon stepped down from the sky, her long hair flickering with pale light.

The Lady Moon looked sadly around the meadow. The rain had battered the pretty meadow flowers and she knew that her gentle light was not bright enough to make the honeysuckle bloom again. As she gazed down at her reflection in the stream, two tears rolled down her cheeks and splashed into the shallow water. Black rings appeared around the tears and grew larger and larger, then disappeared. The Lady Moon could now see another face reflected in the water, a small face with round eyes and long ears! She turned, and stood face to face with Hubert.

"The world can be a sad place," she said, "when it is so cold, so grey and so wet. The harvest is ruined and the people are hungry."

Hubert gazed at the moon and said shyly, "I'm sure the sun would shine if he knew how sad you were."

"I am Queen of the Night," said the moon. "At dawn I fade into the sky and the sun doesn't notice me. Will you take a message to him little hare?"

She slipped her long white fingers into the dark water and grasped the tears. She dropped the tears into Hubert's paws and told him he must take them to the sun, and ask for a bright warm summer. Hubert decided that he really wanted to help. He looked down at the glistening tears, and then turned to ask the moon how to do this difficult task. For a moment, he could not see her. Hubert gazed back up into the sky and there was the moon, round and pale in her rightful place among the stars.

Chapter 4

The Moonstones

Hubert woke with a start. Benedict was preparing breakfast and Petronella was washing her ears.

"I know you young cats do not like greens," Benedict said in a slightly disapproving voice as he carefully arranged fresh clover on a little wooden platter. "So I have collected some eggs, and have prepared them to my own special recipe." The animals settled down to eat and Hubert began to describe what had happened during the night. It was a little difficult to understand his strange tale, partly because he told it with a mouth full of clover. Petronella was amused and explained to Hubert that he had been dreaming.

Hubert felt foolish and looked down at the floor to hide his face. Amongst the leaves and grass at his feet he noticed something shiny. There were the tears of the moon. He picked them up with excitement and showed them to a surprised Petronella. He then turned to Benedict who took the shiny objects and held them up to the light to examine them. Hubert stared at the tears of the moon. He was so fascinated that he did not notice a face looking in at the window.

"These are moonstones," said Benedict, "of the finest quality and of great value. What a wonderful gift for the sun".

Benedict was so busy deciding what to do; he didn't notice the face either.

Petronella, being a practical cat, reminded the two hares that even if Hubert's story was true, which she doubted, delivering the gift would be impossible. There was a noise outside the window, Petronella turned around but didn't see

anything because the face had gone. Benedict looked thoughtfully at Hubert.

"This is indeed an unusual task," he said, "and you are very young and rather small. I wonder why the moon asked you to do something so important."

"I often gaze at the moon," said Hubert, "and the moon likes to be noticed."

"Well, I think you will need our help. We cannot find the sun here, because it is always hidden by clouds. We will have to go on a journey to find the sun. If we are successful in our quest, maybe the sun will shine once more on our land and Petronella's family will be saved."

The animals finished their breakfast and went out into the garden to discuss their plans.

"We need advice," said Benedict. "I am not used to travelling long distances."

A hedgehog snuffled past, his nose close to the damp earth in the hope of finding a juicy worm. Benedict approached the prickly passer-by.

"Excuse me Hedgehog," he said, not getting too close due to the large number of fleas visible among the spines. "I notice that you do not spend the winter in the meadow. Do you travel abroad in the cold season?"

The hedgehog grunted and snuffled.

"No," he replied, "I sleep."

"We are searching for the sun," said Benedict.

"Sun's up in the sky," muttered the hedgehog unhelpfully and continued on his way.

Benedict gazed up into the sky. The hedgehog was right of course, even though he could not see the sun, it was there behind the clouds. As he continued to look at the grey September sky, large numbers of birds were gathering together and circling above the tops of the trees. In a short time, they too would be leaving the meadow. As he stood watching the birds, one of the flock flew down to the stream and caught an insect flying above the water. Benedict took the opportunity of asking the bird where they were going.

"We are going south to find the sun," answered the bird. He swooped back and forth across the stream, his long forked tail almost touching the surface of the water. It is a long flight across land and sea," he sighed, as he flew up to rejoin the flock.

"We must travel south, over the land and the sea," Benedict said, turning to his two young friends.

"The sea?" repeated Hubert.

"Yes, Hubert," replied Benedict, "the sea is a strange place." He pointed towards the stream. "You see how the water runs by the side of the meadow; out beyond the woods it joins a river where the water is wider and deeper. The river flows down to the sea where the water is so wide and so deep that it meets the sky."

Petronella looked alarmed, Benedict reassured her.

"There are boats that travel across the water and reach other lands. We must make our way to the sea and find a boat."

Hubert thought that this was an excellent plan; Benedict must be clever to know about the sea. Petronella didn't seem so sure.

"Come on," said Benedict. "We have lots to do, we must prepare for our journey."

He hurried back into his home with Hubert and Petronella close behind.

They were still unaware that they were being watched. High in the birch tree was a black, beaked face, partly hidden in the shadows, with one eye fixed on Hubert. It was Old Mag, she liked shiny things, and she particularly liked Hubert's moonstones.

Benedict spent the next few hours rummaging through the contents of his little house, gathering together many useful things for their journey, only to find his collection was too heavy to carry. He then spent more time deciding what to take and what to leave behind. Finally, he disappeared out into the garden to gather yet more provisions. Benedict reappeared with armfuls of herbs. He carefully sorted them while the other two watched with interest, but Hubert was getting a bit impatient.

"Why does it take so long to get ready? Why don't we leave now?"

"Nasturtium," said Benedict holding up a bunch of round leaves on thick stems, "very good for aching muscles. Chamomile," he added, arranging the ferny leaves together, "useful for sore feet. Pennyroyal to deter fleas, Rue to prevent plague."

Hubert was having second thoughts, he didn't realise that journeys were so risky. He looked at Petronella's sad face, and remembered the moon's sad face.

"When do we leave?" he asked.

"Tonight at dusk," said Benedict, packing his collection of herbs into a piece of red cloth. "There will just be enough time for you to tell your mother that you have to deliver a message to the sun from the moon, and that you may be gone for some time."

Hubert imagined what his mother would say to this, knowing that mothers do not always take their small children seriously.

It was mid-afternoon when the luggage was finally packed. There was an assortment of small bundles, a walking stick made from a branch of myrtle and a small leather pouch containing the moonstones.

CHAPTER 5

THE JOURNEY BEGINS

The three animals spent the rest of the afternoon sleeping and as the daylight dimmed, Benedict began to wake. He peered out at the sky that was glowing with a pink light behind the dark outlines of the hedgerows. Benedict nudged Hubert who blinked sleepily.

"Look," whispered Benedict, "the evening light shines in the west." He turned away from the light and pointed towards the dark trees. "This means that we must head towards the forest, which is south."

The pink light faded to a glow, then disappeared down behind the undergrowth. The moon was waning, but still looked almost round and gave enough light for the travellers to find their way towards the forest.

They followed a path through groups of sweet chestnut trees. The silence of the woods was broken only by the churring call of the nightjar. Deeper into the forest, the chestnut trees mingled with glades of beech. The ground below was bare but for a sprinkling of damp leaves and twigs. The beech trees loomed over their heads, their black canopy of leaves held high on their colourless ghost-like trunks. The forest grew darker and darker. Hubert heard a flapping noise behind him and a black and white shape flew above his ears and disappeared into a nearby tree. *I wonder what colour dragons are*, he thought to himself, *could they be black and white?* Hubert was frightened but he kept his fears to himself because he did not want to appear foolish in front of the others. He wondered if Petronella was frightened too.

"Are you two all right?" enquired Benedict, looking back at their worried little faces through the gloom.

"Yes," they answered untruthfully.

"Well, you are brave," said Benedict, "as I'm a little afraid myself."

The three continued through the night. They were all relieved as the trees began to give way to grass and they found themselves on a velvety green pasture. In the distance, Hubert could just make out some ghostly shapes lying motionless on the ground. As he approached one of the shapes, it moved. Hubert moved too; quickly in the opposite direction, and came face to face with another strange, pale being. It looked down at him with small black eyes and Hubert looked up at its white eerie face. The little hare quickly glanced around in terror; he could not see Petronella or Benedict. He seemed to be surrounded by the strange phantoms. Hubert was panic-stricken. This was even worse than the dark forest and the flapping wings. He took a deep breath and screamed. The phantoms backed away and began to bleat.

"Have you not seen sheep before?" said a voice behind him. It was Petronella.

Hubert slowly recovered from his fright as he hopped along behind Petronella and Benedict, down into a great valley. A faint light began to appear in the sky, and was reflected in the valley below like a long shiny ribbon.

"Look," said Hubert, "I can see water, is it the sea?"

"It is water," agreed Benedict, "but it isn't the sea. It is the Great River which runs down to the sea in the east." He pointed east to where the sky was becoming lighter and lighter. "We must cross the river and travel south to the sea, the eastern route is too dangerous. The southern route will take us across the marshes. Our scent will not lie on the marshy ground so we cannot be followed by dogs or foxes."

As the sun rose and the birds in the trees began to announce the new day with their singing, the three friends arrived at a bridge. They crossed the river and found themselves on a long straight road.

"This road was built by the Romans many years ago," said Benedict. "It goes all the way to Colchester," he explained, waving his paw behind him. "That way leads to the marshes," he added, pointing to a narrow track.

Hubert wasn't very interested in the Romans, he was far too tired.

Benedict began to look for a safe resting place. Soon, they came upon a little hollow surrounded by tall grass and reeds. The ground was rather damp, but Hubert and Petronella hardly noticed as they curled up in their hiding place.

Benedict looked around him. He could see quite a long way across the flat marshland before it disappeared into the mist. He shivered. When he was young he had travelled around, but he had never been further than the marshes before. He gazed into the mist, wondering what adventures awaited them in the weeks and months ahead.

"Soon we will be in foreign lands," he murmured to his young travelling companions. "Isn't it exciting?"

There was no reply. Benedict, worried by the silence, looked around to see Hubert and Petronella, fast asleep.

Chapter 6

Ranulf the Rat and Eustace the Monk

Benedict, Hubert and Petronella continued their journey across the marshes. They found their way across dykes and reed beds, often turning back to avoid floods where the rain had filled the ditches to overflowing. Eventually, they came to the sea. It was huge, grey and noisy, splashing white foam onto the sand. It wasn't at all like the stream at home, or the river they had crossed. The sea looked as if it went on forever, and all three animals began to feel quite frightened.

As they gazed out to sea, Hubert was suddenly aware of the sound of scampering feet, and to his surprise, he saw a procession of small creatures heading down towards the beach. They were black and furry, with glittering eyes, round ears and long tails.

"Rats!" exclaimed Petronella, preparing to pounce.

"Please, have mercy," cried a voice from the end of the procession.

Hubert looked around to see a slightly larger member of the rat company struggling with a large amount of luggage. Hubert was relieved to see Petronella put away her claws. He stared at the overloaded rat who was accompanied by another, rather fatter, rat wearing a yellow silk handkerchief.

"Let me introduce myself," he continued, putting down his heavy load. "My name is Ranulf, and this," he said, pointing to the wearer of the silk handkerchief, "is my wife Constance, and these," he sighed, waving a paw at the rest of the crowd, "are my children!"

Hubert looked at the large group of children, the large

amount of luggage and the large wife, and began to feel sorry for Ranulf. He was thankful Petronella hadn't eaten him.

"My wife," explained Ranulf, "has a sister who lives in Flanders, and so we go and visit her quite regularly." He pointed to the horizon where the sea meets the sky.

"You cross the sea?" said Hubert with admiration.

"Yes," replied the rat, "we sail with Eustace the Monk."

"Eustace the Monk?" enquired Hubert, who was finding this whole conversation a little confusing.

"Yes, Eustace is a pirate. He sails across the seas and fills his ship with all sorts of interesting things. There's plenty to eat and my wife finds herself clothes of the best quality."

Benedict had been listening to this conversation with great interest.

"Do you think Eustace the Monk would mind if we travelled on his ship too?" he asked.

"No, of course not," reassured Ranulf the rat, "as long as he doesn't know you are there."

Petronella looked uneasy.

"Don't worry," said Ranulf, "I will show you where to hide. A word of warning," the rat's voice dropped to a whisper. "Make sure that you look after any valuables, this place is full of thieves!"

Hubert clasped the leather pouch containing the moonstones. He must be careful not to lose these precious stones or Petronella's family may be lost forever and their journey would be all for nothing.

Ranulf led the way towards the quayside where there were several ships waiting for the wind and tides to take them across the channel. As the company of travellers approached, the quiet of the countryside behind them changed into a noisy bustling throng. Men were hurrying back and forth with wooden caskets and heavy sacks. Fortunately, they seemed too busy to notice the extra passengers arriving on board.

Eustace the Monk had an old wooden ship with raised castles at each end. There was a single mast on which the sailors were busy raising a large square sail. At the top of the mast was the crow's nest, and from the crow's nest you could see everything that was happening below. The cargo had already been loaded and Eustace, who was in quite a hurry to set sail, shouted impatiently at his crew. Ranulf suggested that they hid among some sacks of wool. Petronella agreed. Hubert could not get comfortable and fidgeted about in his sack.

"Keep still," hissed Petronella.

"My wool sack is lumpy," complained Hubert.

Benedict investigated the sack and found not only wool but also two silver goblets, three silver plates and four silver candlesticks! Constance gazed at her reflection in the silver plate and rearranged her silk handkerchief gown.

"Oh Ranulf," she pleaded with her husband, "I have always wanted a full length mirror!"

"Constance," he said, "I don't care if it is a full width mirror, put it back!"

Benedict suggested that everyone should settle down and be quiet as he didn't particularly want to be caught by Eustace the Monk.

Once all the animals were still, they noticed the noise of the waves lashing against the creaking timbers. The wind was moaning above their ears and the ship kept leaning, first one way then the other, as it sailed out to sea. At the top of the mast, inside the crow's nest, sat Old Mag.

CHAPTER 7

TALES OF THE PIPER

Eventually, Eustace the Monk and his ship full of cargo – mostly contraband and stowaways – approached the Flemish coast. It was almost dark when they landed, and the waves lapped onto the shore like black ink. It was quiet, the wind had dropped and the rain had ceased. The moon was high in the sky and Hubert caught glimpses of her between the dark drifting clouds. Benedict helped his companions off the boat, keeping in the shadows and out of view. Ranulf and Constance struggled with their luggage, which looked even heavier than before.

"I hope that package does not contain a silver plate," whispered Petronella to Constance who was having trouble seeing where she was going.

"Of course not," snapped Constance, "it wouldn't fit!"

Constance called to her children to stay close; she was worried that one of them may be at risk of going missing in the presence of a cat. Hubert quickly checked his belongings, worried that something valuable, such as the moonstones, may be at risk of going missing in the presence of a rat. He noticed that the little leather pouch had been tampered with and the knot was loose. In a panic, he untied the knot and looked inside. The moonstones were still there, what a relief! A black and white feather drifted past his whiskers on the cool evening breeze.

All through the night, the shuffling of tiny feet could be heard along the moonlit road. Hubert glanced back at the company of rats; he thought that their footsteps seemed to be

getting louder. He mentioned this to Petronella. He pricked his long ears and listened to the sounds coming out of the darkness. He could hear rustling, muttering, talking, laughing and shouting.

Hubert, Petronella and Benedict stopped and turned to see the family of black rats. Beyond them in the distance, they could just make out a group of brown rats, some grey rats and a few tawny rats. Benedict called for the little army to stop and explain themselves. A large grey rat stepped forward; he spoke in a shrill voice with a strange accent.

"I come from the East. I had to swim a great river to bring you important news. I must warn you to beware of the piper!"

His audience began to mutter to each other.

"Be quiet!" ordered Benedict. "Let him speak".

The grey rat continued.

"I used to live far from here with my brothers and sisters, aunts and uncles, cousins, friends and neighbours in a country called Saxony. One day a stranger arrived in our town. He was dressed in a long ragged gown: red on one side, yellow on the other. Around his waist was a belt, which held a silver flute. He took the flute from his belt and put it to his lips and then I heard…" The rat stared into space, his eyes wide and glittering.

"Yes, and then what happened?" asked Petronella a little impatiently.

The grey rat looked startled. He had not noticed a cat amongst his audience.

"Please continue," said Benedict. "I think we are all friends here."

The rat carried on with his story.

"The strangest music filled the air. We all danced to the tune as the piper played. On and on we danced, across fields, through meadows, we couldn't stop until suddenly..." He paused and shivered. "Suddenly we were all in the river. The water was cold and we were so far from the bank. A few of us just swam and swam until finally we reached the other side."

"What about the others?" asked Hubert.

"Drowned," replied the rat.

There was a stunned silence, and then gradually the muttering and chattering began again amongst the crowd of rats he had met on his travels since that fateful day.

"What happened to the piper?" asked Hubert.

"I never saw him again," said the rat. "But I have heard that we rats were not the only creatures he charmed away. Some of my friends have seen towns and villages with no children. The mothers weep for their lost little ones. Brothers, sisters, big children, small children: all gone. The streets where they played are now silent and empty."

Hubert and Petronella looked at each other in dismay. It seemed that they had arrived in a dangerous and frightening place. Benedict comforted his two young friends.

"We have come too far to turn back and we still have a long way to go."

"I am afraid of the piper," said Petronella. "I am not a good swimmer."

"Don't be frightened," said Benedict. "We know what he

looks like. The rat gave us this warning to help us stay out of danger, not to alarm us."

"I wonder if there are any dragons here," said Hubert suddenly.

Benedict sighed. The two hares and the cat parted company with the rats and headed south towards the sun.

Chapter 8

The Trap

The quest for the sun took the three brave little animals through Flanders and into France. They travelled by night and found shelter, whenever they could, by day. As the weeks went past, the nights grew longer and colder, and finding food was more difficult. One morning, just as the dawn was breaking, Petronella climbed a tree to look for a suitable place to rest. Not too far away she could see the edge of a forest and suggested to Benedict and Hubert that they could hide among the trees until dusk.

They walked towards the forest and took a narrow pathway through the undergrowth. The ground was covered with fallen leaves and the brambles caught at their fur and scratched their ears

Hubert looked up at the trees, he thought that they were watching him and whispering to each other. He stopped and sniffed the air. There was a smell of damp leaves and mushrooms, wild garlic and the tracks of other creatures that lived in the forest. He could also smell something else, but he wasn't sure what it was. Hubert was uneasy. There was something about this forest he did not like. He could smell fear.

With his nose in the air, he didn't see the large white object on the path in front of him, and he accidentally stepped on it. A huge puff of smoke filled the air and, just at that moment, he was knocked sideways by a great winged creature that began to cough and sneeze and make all sorts of other loud, unpleasant noises. The little hare was terrified.

"I stood on that dragon's egg and it hatched," he wailed, running around in circles.

As the smoke settled, Hubert saw the flattened white object lying near his feet, and a very dusty one-eyed magpie glaring at him from the top of a dead tree.

"What is it?" asked Petronella, tapping the egg carefully with one paw before backing away.

"It isn't an egg, it's a puffball," explained Benedict. "A puffball is a type of fungus – like a mushroom or a toadstool."

"Why did it breathe fire?" asked Hubert.

"That wasn't real smoke, although it certainly startled that bird," said Benedict. "The puffball is full of dust, special dust called spores, and from the spores new puffballs will eventually grow."

Hubert sighed. He had been so sure that he could smell danger in the forest, and instead it was only a silly old puffball. He wished that he could be clever like Benedict.

Old Mag was getting very cross as she couldn't remove all the dust from her feathers. She coughed and sneezed and then flew off, leaving a trail of dust on the forest floor.

Benedict led the way up a narrow track through piles of brown leaves and bracken. Suddenly there was a sharp grating noise and a sudden bang. Benedict cried out in pain and, clutching his back leg, stumbled to the ground. Hubert and Petronella looked on in horror as their dearest friend collapsed, his little walking stick and bundle of belongings falling in a heap beside him.

Petronella rushed towards the injured hare and brushed away the leaves. Two curved bands of rusty iron clasped his leg, the jagged edges biting into his flesh. Three drops of bright red blood dripped on to the dead, brown leaves. Hubert felt hot tears spill on to his face and drip down his whiskers.

"We must do something," said Petronella, but for a moment she stood still, unable to do anything.

Hubert started to pull at the trap. The iron jaws refused to move. Then Petronella clawed at the rusty spring, but she did not have the strength to free poor Benedict. The old hare gazed helplessly at his young friends with a faraway expression.

"You cannot stay here. Whoever set this trap will return and you will be in danger. You must take the moonstones and continue your journey alone," Benedict said in a weak, small voice. He looked so very tired and closed his eyes.

"But we can't leave you here," cried Hubert.

Benedict made no reply.

"But we can't leave him here," wailed Hubert, turning to Petronella.

Petronella made no reply.

"I'm not leaving him here," said Hubert, thumping his feet on the ground. "I want to go home," he whimpered. "What are we going to do?"

Petronella gathered up all their belongings and led Hubert away. They continued along the path slowly and silently, looking carefully to see if there were any more traps hidden in the leaves, waiting to snatch their toes or bite their ankles. Hubert suddenly stopped and twitched his ears.

"What is it?" whispered Petronella.

"I can hear footsteps," he said. They hid themselves in the undergrowth and waited. A tall, dark figure appeared out of the shadows. He was dressed in a long brown robe with a large hood that made it impossible to see his face. As he came nearer, they could hear the sounds of twigs cracking beneath his feet. Hubert and Petronella held their breath. The faceless, hooded figure approached their hiding place, but then turned and took another path which led into a clearing.

Hubert and Petronella peered cautiously from behind a group of sapling trees. The man had seated himself on a log. Several of the surrounding trees had been cut down and the light was able to reach this part of the forest. They could see the man quite clearly as he removed his hood and began to talk.

"Who is he talking to?" asked Hubert.

"I don't know," said Petronella, "I can't see anyone else."

As they watched the stranger, they were surprised to see two woodpigeons fly down into the clearing, close to his feet. Moments later, a rabbit and a young deer came forward out of the dark trees beyond. The man beckoned to the deer and it drew near to his hand and rubbed its soft face against the coarse brown cloth of his sleeve. Hubert quietly slipped away from Petronella's side. He crossed the clearing and joined the group of animals assembling on the sunlit grass. Hubert looked into the stranger's eyes – they were dark, kind eyes – and he suddenly felt that this was no ordinary man. Hubert listened to him speak.

"I am Francis, I come from Italy. I have left my home and wealth behind and I live as you do. My bed is the soft grass; my roof is the night sky and my supper, the fruits of the hedgerow."

Francis turned to look at Hubert, he must have been able to see the sorrow in his big brown eyes.

"You look troubled little hare," he said. "Do you need help?"

Hubert turned and slowly went back towards Petronella. Francis followed, and was surprised to see the young hare and his cat companion walking solemnly together along the path. Hubert and Petronella retraced their steps and led Francis to where Benedict lay. Benedict was very still. Francis knelt beside the old hare. Carefully, he forced the iron jaws of the trap apart and released Benedict's injured leg. Still Benedict did not move. Hubert began rummaging around and finally found the leather pouch containing the moonstones. He showed the stones to Francis. Even in the dim light of the forest they shone with a clear blue flame.

"You can't give him those," said Petronella. "They are not yours to give."

"I don't care," said Hubert. "I want Benedict back."

Francis smiled. "You possess treasure of great value," he said, looking at the moonstones. "But they will not bring back a life if it is time for that life to end. All we can do is have faith."

Hubert did not know what faith was, or whether indeed he had any.

Francis picked up the old hare and carefully carried him along a winding path that led to the other side of the forest. The tall brown-robed figure, with his following of creatures, entered a stone building. Petronella gazed at the strange surroundings. It was quite unlike the little cottage where she was born. Inside the walls were white. Shafts of sunlight poured through the coloured glass of the windows making rainbows through the heavily scented air. Candles burned with a steady flame all around them.

Francis put Benedict down gently and gave instructions for the others to watch over him. He left, but returned a few minutes later with a bowl of water, some healing herbs and some linen. He carefully bathed and bound the wounded leg and talked gently to the motionless animal.

Hubert watched the changing patterns of colours on the white walls as the sun slowly moved across the sky, lighting up the coloured glass of the windows. It was, by this time, late afternoon and still the animals kept watch. Finally their patience was rewarded. Benedict opened his eyes. He was alive.

Chapter 9

The Canticle of the Sun

When Francis realised that Benedict had recovered, he was delighted. He spoke to him in a soft but rather stern voice.

"Brother Hare, why did you allow yourself to be deceived like this?"

Benedict looked thoughtful as though he was trying to remember what had happened early that morning. The pathway through the forest was dark and unfamiliar, they had all felt uneasy, but he had been distracted by Hubert and the puffball. Hubert's constant fussing about dragons had made him laugh, but it had also made him careless and he had failed to see the real danger. Even though Benedict was a wise old hare, he was now even wiser.

Benedict looked across at his two companions, Petronella looked tired. She yawned and stretched, then curled up and closed her eyes. She purred with contentment. Hubert, on the other hand, looked remarkably wide-awake. Excitement twinkled in his large brown eyes.

"Are you all right Hubert?" whispered Benedict quietly so as not to disturb the sleeping Petronella.

"Oh yes," said Hubert less quietly. Petronella's ears twitched, but she did not wake. "I think I have found the sun."

"Really?" said Benedict.

"Well," began Hubert, "this afternoon, while you were sleeping, the sun shone through the windows, but it wasn't ordinary sunlight. The sunbeams danced on the walls and changed into every colour of the rainbow. I think the sun

brought you back to life, because he was so pleased with the moonstones."

"You gave the moonstones to the sun?" said Benedict in a very surprised voice.

"Well, no, not exactly," said Hubert. "I left them where he was shining through that open window, and he must have taken them, because they have gone."

Benedict looked concerned. Petronella opened one eye, sighed, and then closed it again. Hubert had expected his friends to be excited by his news and began to wonder whether he had done something wrong.

"Don't worry, Hubert," comforted Benedict. "It has been another very confusing sort of day and we are all very tired. You get some rest, and in the morning the sun will rise and we will find out what to do."

Benedict moved his aching leg into a more comfortable position, and settled down to sleep. In the distance, Hubert could hear Francis chanting a haunting song about his brother sun who brings the day, and his sister moon who brightens the heavens. He felt safe in the strange peace of his surroundings.

Hubert must have slept for a while, because when he next looked up, the brightly coloured sunlight had gone, and soft, silver moonbeams were gliding in through the open door and gently tugging at his ears and whiskers. He got up and wandered out into the night. As he peered through the twilight, he was astonished to see lots of moons. There, in front of him, was a trail of tiny, silvery-white moons disappearing into the distance. They were not up above his ears, shining in the night sky, but down by his feet.

As if in a trance, he followed the trail, straying far into the forest. Everything around him was black and white. He looked up and saw white stars and black treetops, and then he looked down and saw the black ground and the strange, white, moonlike shapes. He looked up again and saw a white cage balanced on top of a black cart. Inside the cage was a black and white bird, and by the bird's feet were two familiar tear shaped drops, glowing in the starlight. Hubert realised his quest was not over yet.

He clambered on to the cart, trying not to wake the sleeping bird. He made his way past the various boxes, baskets and blankets on the cart. He was startled to hear voices behind him.

"Where is he?"

"I don't know, are you sure he got on to the cart?"

The cart lurched forward and Hubert was thrown backwards. The voices cried out as he landed heavily on Benedict and Petronella.

"You followed me", said Hubert, breathing a sigh of relief. "Or did you follow the trail of moons along the path?"

"Moons?" questioned Benedict. "Oh, you mean the puffballs."

"Poor Hubert," said Petronella. "He always gets confused."

"I'm not confused," said Hubert. "It isn't always important to know what things *are*; sometimes you just need to work out what they *mean*. Maybe the moon was sending me a message to help me discover that the moonstones have been stolen, and it looks as though someone else has already caught the thief. Now I will have to try and get them back!"

He looked up at the bird in the cage. Old Mag was now wide awake. She looked at him with one eye. He looked at her long, pointed beak, and sharp, curved claws that were grasping the moonstones.

"There's no hurry," explained Hubert. "I will get the moonstones back later on."

"I wonder who caught the thief," said Petronella.

"Well, we know that someone has been setting traps in the forest, because I was caught in one," said Benedict.

They peered towards the front of the cart and saw a man hunched over the reins of an old donkey. Occasionally the man cracked a small whip across the back of the donkey to force him to pull the cart faster.

"I think we should stay out of sight for the time being," said Benedict.

They all hid among the boxes and blankets on the back of the cart.

CHAPTER 10

THE CHILDREN'S CRUSADE

The cart rumbled on and on, through forests and fields, up hills and down into valleys. Hubert fidgeted around in his hiding place under the blanket and then put his nose in the air and sniffed. He could smell salt water. The cart jolted its passengers up and down as they made their way into a town, past a large signpost on which was painted the name "Marseille".

Hubert and Petronella peered out from the back of the cart. Marseille was quite unlike anything the animals had seen before. The tall buildings hung over the streets and looked just as though they might suddenly topple over. There were lots of people crowding the pavements. Hubert saw street-traders selling pies and pastries, knights in tunics and chain-mail and women carrying babies and baskets of shopping. Suddenly his attention was diverted away from the hustle and bustle of the crowds. His ears twitched and a strange expression came into his eyes. He could hear the distant silvery notes of a flute. It was a haunting sound. Hubert looked across at Petronella. She twitched her ears, perhaps she could hear the same tune.

Hubert and Petronella felt a gentle breeze of sea air ruffle their fur. They could hear the distant sound of waves breaking onto the shore, mixed with the music of the flute. The horizon cleared of houses and carts and in their place a wide expanse of blue water appeared. Hubert gazed at the white foamy edges of the sea rushing forward on to the sand, then falling back again.

At first he thought the music was coming from the waves,

but then he noticed a tall figure standing by the edge of the water. He was dressed in a long, ragged gown, red on one side, yellow on the other.

The cart came to a stop. Without saying a word, Hubert climbed out of the cart and on to the road, closely followed by Petronella and Benedict.

In broad daylight, and with no thought of the danger, they walked down the road towards the sea. The sound of the waves grew louder and louder but still the piper's eerie melody danced in their ears. On and on they went as if in a trance. Then, quite unexpectedly, the music stopped. Hubert looked at Petronella.

"What's happened? Where are we?" he whispered.

"I don't know," said Petronella. She looked confused and frightened.

"We must get back to the cart," said Hubert. "The moonstones are still inside the birdcage."

The animals then realised that they were not alone. Strange faces peered down at them; small faces with staring eyes, unwashed faces with tangled hair. Little hands tried to touch them. Dirty little feet trod on their paws. They were surrounded. There was no escape. Benedict, Hubert and Petronella had found themselves in the midst of a great crowd of children!

On the harbour wall sat two girls and a boy. The smallest girl looked unhappy. Her eyes were dark from lack of sleep and her thin face was tear-stained and smudged with dust from the road. It was late afternoon and the air was cool. The little girl shivered. The elder girl looked at Petronella and beckoned to her.

"Come, puss, my brother and sister will not harm you."

Petronella went up to the children, and the little girl smiled and held out her hand. She jumped up onto the little girls lap. The eldest child was called Adela. She was tall with fair hair and blue eyes. She looked across at her brother Bertran who sat idly kicking the wall with his heels.

"Don't you think we ought to try and find our way home?" she suggested.

"No, we can't give up now," replied Bertran, who was enjoying the adventure more than his sisters. "The piper is leading us on a crusade; we will travel across the sea and join all the crusading knights in a faraway land."

"But how can we cross the sea?" asked Rosa, the youngest of the three.

"The piper will find a way," said her brother, and he turned to watch the crowds of children down by the shore.

"I'm going to find out what's happening," he said, and jumped off the wall.

"Should we go too?" asked Rosa.

"No," replied Adela. "I think we should stay here. I expect Bertran will soon come back."

Bertran looked at his sisters. "I wish I had brothers instead," he muttered to himself as he walked off in the direction of the town.

Meanwhile, the piper had arranged for seven ships to take all the children across the Mediterranean Sea.

Rosa sat very close to Adela and waited. The cold sea air made her fingers and toes tingle and she was glad for the warmth from Petronella, who had curled up on her lap. A little way along, by the wall and sitting in the shadows, were Hubert and Benedict.

"We must find the cart with the birdcage", said Hubert. "I'm surprised Petronella is making herself so comfortable with those children. Why isn't she helping us look for the bird who has stolen the moonstones?"

"Cats are not like us," said Benedict. "We like to be free in the fields and meadows, far away from everyone. Cats like to be with people. They share their firesides and their suppers. I expect Petronella misses Dame Grizel."

At that moment, Hubert caught a glimpse of the two girls disappearing into the crowd, carrying Petronella with them. Hubert hurried down towards the quayside, where the ships were waiting, with Benedict following close behind. They made their way through a forest of legs, not knowing who to search for first: Petronella or the moonstone thief.

CHAPTER 11

SEVEN SHIPS

B y the time Hubert and Benedict reached the quayside, the first three ships were already full and unfurling their sails. Hubert scampered about unnoticed among the children who all wanted to be first to board the next ship. There was so much commotion on the beach at Marseille: Hubert was looking for the birdcage, Benedict was looking for Petronella and trying to keep an eye on Hubert at the same time, Adela and Rosa were looking after Petronella, but had lost their brother Bertran.

Hubert watched as the ships gradually moved one by one away from the shore. On board the second ship, he noticed a small boy making his way across the deck carrying a large cage. The boy waved to two girls on the third ship, one of whom was carrying a small cat.

"Look," cried Hubert, "We are going to have to sail across another sea." Benedict smiled at Hubert.

"You notice things with your young eyes that my old eyes cannot see. What would we do without you?"

Hubert felt pleased. "It's my turn to look after the others," he said to himself. "I won't do anything silly anymore. I shall even try not to worry about dragons."

Hubert stretched his legs, they were definitely getting longer. He smoothed down his ears, they were getting longer too. Hubert was growing up. The two hares crept on board the seventh ship. Hubert hoped that he would be able to find Petronella when they reached land once more.

*

The first few weeks of the voyage dragged by, there was not very much food and water and some of the children were seasick. At night it was cold and they shivered in their ragged clothes, dampened by the spray from the sea. During the day the sun was strong, and there was no shade to protect the children from its burning rays.

"I don't feel at all well," murmured Hubert miserably. "I'm so thirsty, and the sea water tastes disgusting."

"You mustn't drink sea water," said Benedict. "It is too salty – it will make you even thirstier."

"What do fish drink then?" asked Hubert.

"You really need to learn what is best for hares before you start worrying about fish," replied Benedict.

"Do you think that there are such things as sea dragons?" said Hubert. The thought of sea dragons took his mind off the longing he had for a drink.

"No!" said Benedict. Hubert felt thirsty again.

Hubert then noticed one of the crew filling a small leather jug from a large wooden barrel. The sailor put the jug to his lips and drank greedily. He looked around cautiously, and when he was satisfied that no one could see him, he refilled the jug. He was just about to drink for the second time when Hubert heard the loud boom of the captain's voice summoning all hands to the deck. The thirsty sailor dared not disobey and left the jug, still half full, down beside the barrel.

The wind was strong and the ship tilted from side to side. The barrels were tied down securely to prevent them rolling back and forth, but the leather jug slid easily across the damp wooden floor. Hubert watched with interest as the jug slid towards his hiding place. As it came within reach Hubert grabbed the jug. He looked around at Benedict, but the old hare had closed his eyes and Hubert thought it best not to disturb him. Hubert peered down into the jug and sniffed. The liquid was brown and had a strange aroma. This water doesn't look very clean, he thought to himself, but the sailor seemed to like it.

He lapped the liquid. It tasted strange and made his throat feel hot and uncomfortable. When he had finished, he discovered that he still did not feel at all well. His ears felt heavy, but the rest of him felt rather floaty. Then his eyelids felt droopy and he drifted off into a deep sleep.

Hubert slept for a long time; he didn't notice the distant horizon separating the sea and sky widen into beaches and buildings. He didn't feel the warm African sun on his fur. He didn't realise that the crate he and Benedict were hiding in had been taken off the ship, loaded on to a river boat to sail up the River Nile, then unloaded onto the quayside. However, he did notice a sudden, very loud noise.

CHAPTER 12

A REUNION

"What was that?" asked Benedict, turning towards Hubert.

"I don't know," said Hubert, "but it was extremely loud." His poor head ached and his long ears seemed to amplify every sound.

"I don't think I should have drunk the dark water out of the barrel," Hubert said. "It muddled my head and made my ears loud."

"That wasn't water," said Benedict. "That was ale, not at all good for hares, not always good for people either, especially in large quantities. You have grown up a lot in the last few months, but you still have a lot to learn. Listen…there's that noise again. It's a cat."

"Could it be Petronella?" asked Hubert, forgetting his headache for a moment.

"We shall have to go and find out," answered Benedict as he tried to work out from which direction the sound was coming.

The two hares walked slowly along the quayside. They had only recently come ashore and the ground seemed surprisingly still after the swaying of the ship on the sea. Hubert's legs were also a little wobbly as a result of the ale he had drunk and although Benedict's wound had healed after his accident in France, he still walked with a limp.

The quayside was quite busy even though it was late in the day. Hubert caught sight of Adela, Rosa and Bertran all sitting together. It looked as though they were waiting for someone.

Rosa was sleeping with her head resting on Adela's shoulder. Next to Rosa was a basket, and behind the basket was a birdcage. The sun was slowly sinking and the sky painted pink and yellow reflections on the blue water of the River Nile. The moon appeared above them and the noise and bustle of the market place gradually disappeared into silence. There was even silence from the basket beside Rosa. No one had noticed Benedict and Hubert join the weary little group. No one, that is, except Petronella who peeped through the gaps in the wicker work and with relief, saw her two friends again.

"Why are you in that basket?" whispered Hubert.

"We have all been bought by the Sultan of Egypt," replied Petronella.

"I didn't know you were for sale," said Hubert.

"I wasn't," hissed Petronella.

"Shhhh," interrupted Benedict. "We don't want to attract attention."

Petronella continued her story quietly.

"These children have been tricked into leaving their homes and families. They have walked for miles with hardly any food and not much rest. They thought that they were going on an exciting adventure, but instead they were sold as slaves, and will have to work in the Sultan's palace."

"What about the bird?" said Benedict.

"She's a magpie," said Petronella. "The Sultan believes she has magical powers and has bought her for his collection of birds from other lands."

Old Mag sat hunched in her cage, she looked miserable.

"If she had magical powers, she would have disappeared from that cage," said Hubert.

"You're quite right," said Benedict.

"I'm surprised the Sultan didn't think of that," said Hubert, trying to look casual even though he was secretly pleased with himself.

"Now that you are here, could you help me to get out of this basket?" said Petronella.

"Of course," said Benedict, reaching for the peg that was holding the lid down securely.

"Wait," whispered Hubert, "I need to talk to the magpie first, and she might be alarmed if she sees a cat."

Hubert looked at Old Mag. She still looked rather fierce, but Hubert was feeling more sure of himself as he had just thought of a plan to recapture the moonstones. He went right up to the cage and put his paw on a large metal bolt that secured the cage door. He looked up at Old Mag; she put her head on one side and looked back at Hubert.

"I think I could undo that bolt," he said.

"Show me," she replied.

"Not until you give me back the moonstones," said Hubert.

"If I give you the moonstones, you might run off with them and leave the door locked" said Old Mag. She put her face up against the bars of the cage and peered closely at Hubert. The children sitting nearby began to fidget, and then they heard the sound of approaching footsteps.

"You don't have much time to make up your mind," said Hubert, moving the bolt slightly with his paw.

Suddenly, Old Mag tossed the moonstones through the bars of the cage. Benedict picked them up and put them carefully back into the little leather pouch he was carrying as Hubert slid back the bolt. The door swung open and there was a great flurry of black and white feathers as Old Mag made her escape high into the sky and disappeared from view. Hubert and Benedict turned to see the children being led down the road by a tall Egyptian man. Clasped tightly in Rosa's hand was the basket, and inside the basket was Petronella.

CHAPTER 13

EGYPT

The children's crusade had now ended in Egypt, and Adela, Rosa and Bertran were about to begin new lives as slaves in the palace of the Sultan.

The Sultan was a good master. He knew that contented slaves would serve him better than those who were unhappy. On arrival at the palace, the basket was placed in a shady area of the courtyard and the children were told to go and wash in the waters of the Nile before being presented to their new master.

Petronella scratched at the lid of her basket and soon attracted some attention. She was aware of movement in the courtyard, but could not hear the gentle padding of paws getting closer. She thought she could hear sniffing – could it be Benedict or Hubert? Nervously she peeped through the wicker work. Her eyes were met by an inquisitive stare. They were not the dark brown, gentle eyes of a hare. She was being observed by the glassy, amber coloured eyes of another cat. The peg holding the lid of the basket closed fell to the stone floor with a clatter and the lid creaked open.

Three Egyptian cats sat in front of her. Their coats were a warm reddish brown, like autumn leaves, but their faces and tails had tabby markings just like her own. Petronella wondered if they were friendly. She looked up shyly at the tallest of the three cats. He looked back at Petronella.

"Welcome to the palace of Sultan al-Adil," he announced. "Are you alone, or are there more?"

"I have come here with Benedict and Hubert," Petronella answered timidly.

"Ah, so there are three cats who wish to see the Sultan of Egypt," said the second cat.

"Well, no, not really," said Petronella. "Benedict and Hubert are hares, and we haven't come to see the Sultan, we have come to see the sun."

The first cat looked at Petronella curiously. He twitched his whiskers and tilted his head as if to get a better view of this strange new arrival.

Petronella decided to tell them the whole story, after all, they were cats and would, she hoped, be sympathetic to the predicament of her poor relations.

"In my country," she began, "cats are blamed for bad weather. So when the rain and storms ruined the harvest, our cats were imprisoned."

Petronella then continued her story with details about Hubert's meeting with the moon, the gift of moonstones for the sun, and how the moonstones were lost and then found.

One of the Egyptian cats bowed his head thoughtfully as he considered Petronella's story. He paused a moment longer, then spoke,

"I believe that you may soon come to the end of your journey. I, Bellayl, will guide you in your quest, as will my brothers." He nodded at the two cats sitting at either side of him. They nodded back their agreement. Bellayl turned back to Petronella.

"Your river journey on the Nile would have taken you past the ancient city of Heliopolis, the City of the Sun. Two thousand years ago it was the richest city in the land. By day the sun god, Ra, poured his golden light upon Heliopolis. By night the sun's rays were held in the cats' eyes and they shone through the darkness."

"We should go back to find the city of Heliopolis," suggested Petronella with excitement.

"Alas, now the city lies in ruins," said Bellayl. "To search for Ra, the ancient god of the sun, we must go to Giza." Bellayl looked across the Nile to where the evening sunlight reflected on the triangular faces of the pyramids of Giza.

"I, Bellayl, and my brothers will lead you to the great pyramids. But first," he continued, "should we not look for your companions?"

"Oh yes, of course," said Petronella, feeling rather silly. She had been so captivated by the splendour of her surroundings and the charm of her new acquaintances that, for a moment, she had completely forgotten Benedict and Hubert. She looked back towards the palace gates; in the distance she could see two pairs of long ears.

"I will go and fetch them on my own," explained Petronella. "They are rather nervous of large quantities of cats."

CHAPTER 14

THE GREAT PYRAMID

The animals began their expedition to Giza late the following day. By this time, Hubert and his friends were so used to travelling by boat, that finding a hiding place on a Nile ferry wasn't very difficult. When they reached the far bank, Bellayl led the procession along the edge of the river.

They hadn't gone far when Hubert noticed a disturbance in the water below. He leant over to have a closer look when, to his surprise, a large scaly head emerged from the river. The monster's eyes bulged out from the top of his head and glanced greedily at Hubert. Hubert then watched the great jaws open to reveal an enormous row of glistening white teeth, shaped like one hundred small daggers. Before he realised what was happening, he felt the scruff of his neck being grabbed firmly. His feet left the ground and he was dragged away…by Benedict.

"Are you all right?" asked Petronella, as Benedict sat the young hare down some distance from the water's edge.

"Oh it was only a dragon," he said casually.

"It was a crocodile," said Bellayl, "and you were very lucky not to be eaten."

Hubert ignored this identification of the creature. He was sure it was a dragon.

They all continued on their way, each of them glancing occasionally at Hubert. Hubert trotted along quite happily, not at all disturbed by his lucky escape.

"I've seen a dragon," he said quietly to himself. "I've seen a dragon, and it didn't eat me, and it wasn't even as big as I thought it would be. Can't see what all the fuss is about."

"What are you whispering about?" asked Benedict.

"Nothing," said Hubert.

"Well make sure you keep up with us," said Benedict. "You have got the moonstones and this is the most important part of the whole journey."

They could see the pyramids ahead of them rising up out of the desert sands. From the banks of the Nile, the pyramids did not look very big, but as they walked on and on, the pyramids seemed to grow and grow. It was not until they reached the foot of the Great Pyramid that they realised the true size of these mountains of stone.

Benedict looked up at the pyramid. The top seemed to disappear into the darkening evening sky. He turned to Bellayl.

"Do we have to climb right to the top of the pyramid to find the sun?" he asked. "You see, I don't think I could even manage to climb on to the first stone step. I know that you cats are expert climbers, but we hares simply aren't built for it."

"Please don't concern yourself," said Bellayl. "We don't have to find our way to the top, we simply have to find our way inside."

"Is the sun inside?" asked Hubert. "No wonder the pyramid is so large, and no wonder it is so dark out here!"

Bellayl instructed the rest of the group to follow him, as he was the only cat there who knew about the secret passageway. Bellayl stood with his back to the Great Pyramid and took twenty-four paces. On the ground there was a group of stones. He removed some of the stones, and began to dig in the sand.

His brothers joined in the activity and soon there was quite a large heap of soft sand behind them. After a while, Bellayl's paws hit against something hard. Carefully, they cleared the remaining sand to reveal a trapdoor. The trapdoor was opened and a dark passageway appeared, leading back towards the pyramid.

Bellayl led the way down beneath the desert sands. It was extremely dark but the cats were able to find their way through the blackness with the hares following closely behind. At the end of a very long passageway, they reached a second door.

"Be careful as you step over the threshold," warned Bellayl. "Do not touch the walls."

"Why not?" whispered Hubert.

"The ancient Pharaohs of Egypt protect their property from intruders and thieves. This entrance to the pyramid is only the width of my whiskers and the gentle footstep of a cat will not provoke the Pharaoh's curse."

"What curse?" whispered Hubert.

"The heavy fall of a human foot," continued Bellayl, "and the width of his shoulders brushing against the walls would cause the sand to move and the passageway to cave in."

Hubert held in his rounded stomach as he gently placed his foot over the threshold. They found themselves in a small, dark chamber. On the opposite side was a large stone. With difficulty, Bellayl rolled the stone to one side, revealing the entrance to another passage. The floor was sloped and they began an uphill climb to reach the other end.

In single file they crept along the dark, dusty corridor. The air was black, like smoke, and made their eyes water and their throats sore. It was with relief that they noticed the tunnel widening, and they found themselves in a huge chamber.

"I think I've gone blind," said Hubert, rubbing his dusty eyes with his equally dusty paws.

"I'm sure you're not blind," said Petronella, trying to comfort him.

"But if the sun is in here," said Hubert, "I should be able to see it."

Benedict opened his mouth to explain, but he had no explanation to give. Surely the sun had not really set within the walls of the Great Pyramid, and yet if it hadn't, why were they here?

As they all stared into the darkness, they were suddenly aware of a strange noise. It was a jingling, rattling, metallic, musical sound.

CHAPTER 15

HEY DIDDLE DIDDLE

Petronella looked up to the ceiling of the chamber. There was a gentle glowing light, shining above their heads. The light was in the shape of a circle, and looked just like the full moon. The jingling rattling sound became louder and the moon-shaped light grew larger and brighter. Behind the light, appeared the shining eyes and whiskery face of a cat.

"Bow your head," whispered Bellayl to Petronella. She obeyed, but only for a moment. Soon she was overcome with curiosity and glanced up at the approaching figure.

"Who is it?" asked Petronella, but before Bellayl could answer, the figure herself spoke.

"I am Bastet. Welcome to the Great Gallery of the pyramid of Khufu."

They gazed in awe at Bastet. She stood upright, much taller than any cat they had seen before. On her chest she wore a golden ornament in the form of a winged scarab beetle carrying the sun disc. In one paw she carried a musical instrument called a systrum. The systrum was round and shiny like the moon. Attached to the sides of the systrum were horns, just like the horns of a cow. Between the horns were four bars on to which were threaded metal discs. As Bastet waved the systrum above their heads, the metal discs jingled together and filled the chamber with strange music. At the feet of Bastet sat four tiny kittens.

Hubert watched the systrum as Bastet waved it first to one side, then to the other. As he watched, he thought that he could see another pair of horns appear in the dim light of the chamber. The second pair of horns were much larger than those of the systrum. Soon Hubert realised that they belonged to a creature much larger than Bastet. Another, much lower voice spoke to the visitors.

"I am Hathor. Welcome to the Great Gallery of the pyramid of Khufu."

Hubert looked up. There in front of him he saw an enormous cow.

Hubert, Benedict, Petronella and the Egyptian cats simply stood and watched in silence as Bastet the cat continued to play her music, and Hathor the cow pranced and danced around and around. The music became faster and faster as Bastet waved the systrum wildly above her head. Hathor leapt up and down, her hooves pounding on to the stone floor of the Great Gallery. Suddenly she jumped so high, she flew over the head of Bastet and over the top of the shiny moon-shaped systrum. As she landed the ground shook, then everywhere was quiet, Hathor's dance was over and the music stopped.

The silence was then broken by the sound of laughing. Benedict looked at the others. Hubert sat completely still, the cats were also quiet. Still they could hear laughing. Bastet and Hathor were then joined by a third figure, obviously amused by the antics of the cow. He faced the audience of hares and cats with a wide grin.

"I am Anubis. Welcome to the Great Gallery of the Pyramid of Khufu."

Hubert looked up at Anubis, then promptly hid himself behind Petronella. He had been a little nervous of Bastet, simply because of her size, but he had become used to cats. Hathor also made him feel slightly afraid, she was so very large, but he knew that cows eat grass, not hares.

Anubis however was the most frightening of the three. Anubis was a dog. He had a long, thin, black nose and long, thin, black ears. He looked at the visitors with bright, staring eyes, and when he laughed, Hubert noticed lots of sharp, white teeth. Anubis spoke for a second time.

"I am the Royal Guard of the pyramid. Why have you come? Was it to hear Bastet play, or to see Hathor dance?"

Bellayl stepped forward to answer Anubis, "My friends have travelled many miles. They have brought a gift for the sun."

"A gift for the mighty Ra," said Anubis. "What gift could you possibly have for the sun?"

Hubert opened the leather pouch and produced the moonstones. Anubis looked at the stones, and then looked up at the three travellers.

"Where did these come from?" he asked.

"They are a gift from the moon," replied Hubert.

Anubis walked slowly past Benedict, Petronella and all the other cats, staring at each of them in turn. Then he swung around.

"And which one of you has been to the moon?" he asked.

Hubert decided to be brave. After all he had had a close encounter with an Egyptian river dragon, otherwise known as a Nile crocodile. He took a step forward.

"Is it you?" said Anubis, pointing his long nose at Hubert.

Hubert took a step backwards.

"Well, I didn't go to the moon really," he explained. "The moon came to me."

Anubis grinned and showed his gleaming white teeth. He listened as Hubert retold his strange meeting with the moon in a quiet, quivering voice. Hubert was worried that Anubis would not believe him. He wondered what would happen to him if Anubis thought his story was untrue.

Anubis put his head on one side and looked at the young

hare. Bastet and Hathor looked too as Hubert trembled at the amount of attention he was attracting. After a while, Anubis spoke again.

"Come with me, my little moon-gazing hare. We will make an offering to the sun."

Anubis led Hubert through a doorway into another chamber. As the others followed on behind, Hubert stopped and looked around. The walls of the chamber were so tall that it was impossible to see the ceiling. As he glanced upwards, he caught sight of a single massive eye staring back down at him. He found that he could not look away as the eye watched him, unblinking.

"Greetings, Lord of the Skies," said Anubis. "I present three travellers who have journeyed from a distant land. Their fields and meadows are cursed with storms and rain. The Lady Moon begs you to visit their skies and bring life and warmth to their country."

The huge eye of Ra looked down upon the company below.

"Can he hear us?" asked Hubert. "All I can see is one eye."

"Silence," commanded Anubis. "The great Ra has many forms. Offer him your gift."

Hubert held the moonstones high in his paws. The great eye of Ra continued to stare at Hubert. The inquisitive hare stared back at the eye. Suddenly, Hubert was dazzled by a flare of white light. The eye had changed into a golden disc, and the intense brightness caused everyone to look away, their eyes hurting from the unexpected brilliance of the light.

Gradually the light faded enough for Hubert to look up. He saw that the golden disc had become smaller and below it stood a figure with the body of a man and the head of a bird. Around his neck was a jewelled collar glistening with coloured flames. He looked down at Hubert and the moonstones, and then he spoke.

"I have searched the deserts for treasures such as these. Every morning I rise early and gaze long and hard upon this hot, dry earth, hoping to find rare jewels of light, but it seems I have been looking in the wrong place. The eye of Ra must look beyond the scorched deserts to distant lands. I will burn through the rain clouds and warm the fields and meadows that lie across the seas. Go home little hare, you have found what you were looking for, and so have I."

The mighty Ra reached down for the moonstones and placed them into his glistening collar. There was another dazzling flash of light, and Hubert hid his eyes from the glare.

Chapter 16

The City

Petronella mewed in pain as she tried to cover her eyes with her paws. Benedict closed his eyes and turned away. They waited. Benedict, Hubert and Petronella opened their eyes to find themselves in a dark underground chamber.

"I can't see," said Hubert in distress.

"Neither can I," said Benedict, looking desperately into the blackness.

Petronella and the other cats, however, had noticed the smallest glimmer of light coming through the open doorway. Bellayl led the cats back through the Great Gallery of the pyramid, and down into the steeply descending corridor.

Benedict followed Petronella, and Hubert followed Benedict. Then Hubert stopped following Benedict, stood completely still in the darkness and let out a long, loud cry that echoed all around.

"What is it?" asked Benedict

"We've done it!" cried Hubert. "We have crossed the sea, travelled through forests, fields and towns, crossed the sea again, given the sun a gift from the moon, and here we are in a pyramid!" He paused for a moment, then in a quieter voice said, "I wonder how we are going to get home?"

"I hope we are not too late," said Petronella. "It has taken us months to reach the sun, what if something has happened to my family while I was away?"

Bellayl thought for a moment as he remembered Petronella's tale about the cruel miller.

"If the miller really thought that your mistress, the dame,

and her cats had enough power to change the weather, he would not risk harming them."

"Quite right," said Benedict.

Hubert was still wondering how they were going to get home. He was very tired, but he didn't really want the adventure to end.

As they came out of the secret entrance to the pyramid, the dawn was breaking. A passing camel blinked in disbelief as he saw four cats and two hares suddenly emerge from the sand as if appearing from thin air.

The journey back to Cairo was hot and exhausting. They stopped and rested by the Nile, spending the warmest part of the day in a cool hiding place, down by the water. Bellayl kept watch while the others drank. A crocodile was not the only danger to the unsuspecting visitor. Occasionally, a hippopotamus would raise its huge head above the water and open its jaws very wide – wide enough for a young hare to fall in and never be seen again.

When they arrived back on the Eastern bank of the Nile, they saw a group of carts and caravans.

"Look," said Hubert, whose tired feet were still sore from the hot sand. "We travelled by cart in France. Maybe we could have a ride at least part of the way home."

"We don't know where they are travelling to," said Benedict. "It's no good taking a ride in a cart if it is going in the wrong direction."

As they trotted wearily back towards the city, several more carts passed by them on the road. There were carts full of carpets and rolls of silk and linen. Others held various pieces of pottery: tall, thin pots with narrow necks; short, fat pots with wide necks; jars of different sizes; plates and cups.

"They are merchants who come to the city to sell their wares," said Bellayl, dodging the wheels of a particularly wide cart carrying many baskets. "They will set up their stalls for several days, until their goods are sold. Then they will return to their own countries. We need to find out if any of them are travelling back to Europe."

Hubert sniffed the air. All sorts of strange scents caught his attention as he walked along the narrow lanes of the spice bazaar. All around him were tiny booths stocked with bottles of essences, bags of spices, herbal medicines and exotic perfumes. After the spice bazaar came the tent-makers' stalls, with rolls of bright stripy canvas, saddles, bridles, colourful tin lamps and rat-traps.

It was getting late in the day and the sun sank lower in the sky. As they turned the corner, the long evening shadows disappeared into a haze of light from a thousand lamps. Bellayl, who was leading the way, turned to the group.

"Hubert, I think it could be dangerous for you and Benedict to be out in this part of the city. There are always cats and dogs wandering around the alleyways, but not hares. Stay in the shadows – my brothers will show you where to hide – and Petronella and I will try to find a cart that is going back to Europe."

Bellayl and Petronella walked on past the tent-makers' stalls. All the rolls of coloured, stripy canvas were neatly stacked on a low table, and several tin lamps were hanging on a long string above. However, one little tin lamp had been forgotten – it had fallen into the dusty street. Petronella looked at the lamp and rubbed away the dust with her paw.

"I wish we could all be back home in England," she said. The evening air was stirred by a cool breeze and the shutters rattled against the windows. Then all was quiet.

"Come on," said Bellayl. "It's no good wishing."

CHAPTER 17

WULFRIC THE DOG

Meanwhile, Hubert and Benedict stayed out of sight. Bellayl's brothers had gone back to the palace, so the two hares were all alone and feeling rather uncomfortable.

"I don't like the city," said Benedict. "It's too noisy. I prefer the quiet fields and meado–."

He was interrupted by the sudden arrival of a very large, hairy dog, which appeared from nowhere, rushed straight at Hubert, and knocked him over. Hubert cried out in terror. Benedict began to strike the dog with his walking stick, but Hubert knew that they wouldn't be able to defend themselves against such a large animal. Hubert took in a deep breath and yelled, "STOP," as loudly as he could, right into the dog's ear.

"Eh, what's that?" said the dog.

"Stop," repeated Hubert, although by this time the dog had already stopped and was just standing there, looking down on the two hares with a confused expression on his face.

"Oh, I'm sorry, I didn't hear you," said the dog. "My ears don't work as well as they used to. In fact, I didn't even see you there; my eyes are not as good as they used to be either."

Petronella and Bellayl must have heard Hubert's screams as they came rushing back, only to find Hubert deep in conversation (in a loud voice) with an elderly, enormous Irish wolfhound.

"I am looking for my master, but I seem to have lost him, or maybe he has lost me, I'm not sure," said the dog.

"Well if you tell us who you are and where you are from,

maybe we can help you," said Hubert, who was now feeling rather sorry for the unfortunate dog.

"My name is Wulfric," he said. "I have spent many years in many countries, travelling with my master, Sir Baldwin de Bravesby."

"Baldwin," said Bellayl, "that doesn't sound like an Egyptian name."

"It isn't," agreed Wulfric. "My master is from England."

"England," repeated Petronella, "that is where we come from too."

"Do you really," said Wulfric with interest. "I have never been there myself, what is it like?"

"It rains a lot," said Petronella.

"My master left England many years ago, as a young Knight Templar. Now my master is getting old he cannot fight any more, so he is going home. He is travelling with a group of knights whose battle days are over too. They are all returning to England. The trouble is," he said sadly, "I think they have gone without me." He sniffed a few times then lay down. Hubert looked at his droopy head and sorrowful eyes.

"When did you last see your master?" asked Hubert.

"Eh, what's that?" Wulfric lifted his head and twitched one ear. Hubert repeated the question a little louder.

"Well," said Wulfric, trying to concentrate. He scratched his ear and paused. "I think Sir Baldwin was going to the tentmakers. Yes, that's right. He was going to order some tents to provide shelter for the journey." Wulfric looked pleased with himself for remembering, because his memory wasn't what it used to be.

"Didn't we pass the tentmaker's bazaar a little while ago?" said Petronella, remembering the rolls of striped canvas and the coloured tin lamps.

"Yes, that's right," said Bellayl. "We will go back the way we came."

"If we can find your master, do you think we would be able to travel back to England in his cart?" said Benedict.

"Of course you can," said Wulfric. "Sir Baldwin does not travel light. There is always so much stuff in the cart; it won't be difficult to find you all a hiding place."

"What does your master look like?" asked Hubert, as they walked along the passageway that led back towards the tentmaker's stall. Wulfric described Sir Baldwin in some detail to his new friends.

He was not very tall, and not very fat. His grey beard was long, with a hint of a curl. He wore a white mantle with a large red cross on the back. His helmet was rounded at the top and had a dent in the back, of about the size and shape of a large paw. The dent in the back of Sir Baldwin's helmet did have a connection with Wulfric's failing eyesight.

Not long after Wulfric had told them all about his master, an aged knight was seen approaching on a grey horse. Wulfric's tail wagged with such vigour, he was soon hidden in a cloud of dust. Following Sir Baldwin along the road towards the tent-maker's bazaar was a group of travellers, another horse, and a large wooden baggage wagon. The sides of the wagon were made from a series of upright posts, held together with long, horizontal planks of wood. At the top of the upright posts hung a water bucket and some cooking pots. The pots banged together as the wheels of the wagon turned along the uneven road.

When they arrived at the tentmaker's, Sir Baldwin de Bravesby and the other old soldiers were busy inspecting the tents that they had ordered. The wagon was at the side of the lane. Its clanking pots and pans were silent as the horse stood quite still, waiting for the new tents to be loaded on to the back. Wulfric was so pleased to see his master again that the old dog forced his tired old legs to run and greet Sir Baldwin. Sir Baldwin threw up his hands in delight.

"Where have you been, you old scoundrel?" he cried. He gently ruffled the hair on Wulfric's head and ears. "I thought I had lost you forever." The other old soldiers joined in welcoming Wulfric back.

While Wulfric was receiving all this attention, Bellayl took the opportunity to help Petronella, Benedict and Hubert into the wagon. They scrambled through the piles of wooden boxes and scratchy old baskets until they reached a corner that was full of woollen rugs and old blankets.

"Have a safe journey," whispered Bellayl. Two ears and a whiskery nose appeared from within the folds of a multi-coloured rug. It was Petronella. She looked at Bellayl with sorrowful green eyes from her hiding place on the wagon. It was as though she wanted to stay and wanted to go home, all at the same time.

Sir Baldwin and his companions then began to load the tents on to the back of the wagon. Wulfric looked at Bellayl who was waiting a short distance away. Bellayl mewed just loudly enough for Wulfric to hear, and Wulfric knew that this meant his passengers were safely aboard and hidden from view.

Bellayl turned and walked slowly back towards the Sultan's palace alone. Sir Baldwin saw Bellayl and looked at Wulfric.

"Didn't you see that cat, my old friend?" he said to his dog as he helped Wulfric clamber on to the back of the wagon. "A few years ago, you would have given chase. Too old and tired now."

The journey took many months. There were weeks of bumpy wagon rides over rutted roads and rough tracks. In between were the sea crossings: churning and choppy, damp and dismal. On bad days, Petronella tried to cheer herself up by talking about Bellayl and how much she had enjoyed her brief visit to the Sultan's Palace. Benedict just talked about his own comfortable home by the stream, and Hubert wondered what home was really like. He had been to so many places in his short life, he had no clear memory of the place where he was born.

Many nights along the way were spent at Templar convents where Sir Baldwin and his knights were given comfortable beds and a good meal. Even old Wulfric was given a plate of scraps or a juicy bone. The scraps he enjoyed, the bones were rather a struggle. His teeth were not what they used to be. Actually, many of his teeth were not where they used to be, they were completely missing.

While the men were enjoying their food and wine, Hubert and Benedict feasted too. There were plenty of new spring plants with tasty buds and leaves. Petronella went hunting in the surrounding countryside, being careful to return to the wagon well before the journey began again. Sometimes it was too far between convents and Wulfric and his master would sleep under the canvas tents that they had bought in Cairo.

Spring turned into summer as the wagon rumbled through the changing countryside. The hot sands of Egypt were far behind. The waving palm trees of the Mediterranean were replaced by poplars and willows. Instead of scarab beetles and rivers of crocodiles, there were ladybirds and streams of dragonflies. Their surroundings were new and interesting to Wulfric, but they were familiar and comforting to Benedict as they eventually arrived on the shores of old England.

CHAPTER 18

MORE CATS AND ANOTHER HARE

Soon after arriving back in England, Benedict, Hubert and Petronella parted company with Wulfric and his little army of old Crusaders. Wulfric wasn't sure exactly where he was going, but Benedict thought it was unlikely to be the same part of the country to which he, Hubert and Petronella were returning.

"Goodbye, old fellow," said Hubert, as Wulfric lowered his head so that his deaf old ears could hear him. "I hope you will be happy in your new home."

Wulfric raised his head and looked at the summer meadows full of flowers and the broad green trees filled with songbirds.

"I think that I will like it here. Although I expected it to be raining," said Wulfric, remembering Petronella's description of England. There was not a rain cloud in sight. The sun was surrounded by a wide expanse of blue sky.

"I expect it will rain sometimes," said Petronella.

"But the sun will shine," said Hubert confidently, "because we presented him with a gift from the moon."

Wulfric looked at Hubert in a strange way.

"We are grateful for your help," said Benedict to Wulfric. "I sometimes wondered if I would ever see my old home again."

"I am grateful for your help," said Wulfric. "Without it, I might never have seen my old master again."

Hubert, Petronella and Benedict headed north. They crossed meadows and streams, and followed woodland pathways and rough cart-tracks. It was Benedict who first noticed a few familiar trees and heard the soft whisper of a running stream.

Even though they were so very tired, Hubert and Petronella couldn't help running along the banks of the stream, whose clear waters were racing towards home. The meadow grasses were tall and waved their feathery heads in the breeze. White ox-eye daisies and blue cornflowers nodded their welcome to the returning travellers. A pair of butterflies danced in the air

above their ears as Benedict and Hubert came within sight of the old cart house. It was almost hidden by honeysuckle blooms and the bees buzzed excitedly through the fragrant branches.

"Can we go to the cottage first?" asked Petronella.

Benedict looked with longing at his home. The cartwheel garden was overgrown, and would need attention as soon as possible.

"Yes, you're right of course," he said. "We must find out what has been happening here while we were away."

As they crossed the meadow, the cottage could just be seen beyond the hedge, among the trees.

"There's no smoke from the rooftop," said Petronella.

"Well, it is rather warm for a fire today," said Hubert.

"Yes, of course," said Petronella, still a little worried. The door of the cottage was open, and the three animals cautiously crept up to the doorway, and peeped inside.

"There's nobody here," said Petronella, a little more worried.

"Maybe they are in the garden," said Hubert.

They walked down the path towards the vegetable plot. Hiding amongst the peas and beans was Bartholomew. He jumped out from his hiding place, startling the two hares.

"Bless me! Barty, what a bad cat," exclaimed a voice. It was Dame Grizel; she had noticed the visitors arriving and picked up the struggling Bartholomew before he frightened them away. She looked at the two hares, and then she noticed the young tabby cat looking up at her.

"It can't be," she said to herself, looking a little closer at the new arrival. "It is! It is Petronella!" she cried almost dropping the wriggling Bartholomew in surprise. "It has been so long, almost a year, where have you been?"

Petronella rubbed her face against the old woman's skirts. Then, from behind the fruit trees, Maurice and Mortimer appeared and ran up the path to see what was happening.

Petronella was so excited to see her brothers again, she quite forgot about Hubert and Benedict.

"Come on," whispered Benedict. "Let's leave Petronella to her happy reunion. Maybe we will see her again later."

The hares quietly left the welcoming party and returned to the meadow.

"So much has happened since you went away," said the dame to Petronella. "The miller locked my poor cats in a barn. I was so worried. I thought that I would never see any of you again. Fortunately, the miller's wife heard their cries, and although the planks that barred the doors were too heavy for her to lift, she was able to pass a small dish of milk under the door.

"She told me that the miller was in such a bad temper. There was not enough wheat for the winter and the only grain he had kept disappearing from the barn."

The dame went into the cottage and found some scraps for her cats to eat. She went on with her story as she poured a little milk into a bowl for Petronella. Bartholomew helped her to drink it.

"Of course," continued the old woman, "the barn was overrun with mice and rats, and that is why the grain disappeared so quickly. My good boys soon solved that problem."

Petronella glanced over to the hearth. The ashes from the fire lay on the stones, cold and grey. The cosy corner where her mother used to sleep was empty. Dame Grizel still continued chattering.

"As you might expect, the miller and his wife were so pleased with the cats for catching all the mice and rats. They wanted to keep them, but the miller's wife knew that I was so lonely here in my cottage. They agreed to allow Bartholomew, Maurice and Mortimer to return home."

Petronella tried to look pleased, but was still disappointed to find part of her family still missing.

"Your dear mother," said the dame, "decided to stay with the miller's wife. She now has five new kittens; a little black girl and four naughty tabby boys. You may visit them whenever you wish." Petronella gave a quiet purr, finished her milk and trotted towards the open door.

"A word of warning," added the old woman. "The miller himself is still rather bad tempered. You see, the spring and summer has been so warm that he has the most terrible sunburn, especially on his nose."

*

Hubert and Benedict walked slowly back across the meadow.

"Well done Hubert," said Benedict. "Petronella is with her family again." As they approached the stream, Hubert noticed a pair of black tipped, brown ears just above the tops of the feathery grasses. He went over to have a closer look. Through the forest of stalks and leaves, he could just see a second pair of black tipped, brown ears, smaller and a little lower down than the first pair.

"Do many other hares live in this meadow?" he asked Benedict, still peering through the undergrowth to catch a glimpse of the owners of the ears.

"Why yes," said Benedict. "We hares have lived in these parts for generations. You left your home at such a young age, I suppose there was no time for you to meet them."

As they came nearer, Hubert could see that one of the hares was quite small, probably not very old. He stopped. The two other hares seemed quite unaware that he was there. Hubert listened. He heard a familiar voice.

"Soon you will be old enough to explore the meadow on your own, but you must take care. Beware of the cat, the dog and the dragon. If you lie still they may not see you. If they see you, you must run swiftly."

Hubert's eyes widened, then became misty. There was a pause, and then a small voice asked, "What is a cat, a dog and a dragon?"

Benedict and Hubert began to listen to the explanation given by the mother hare.

"She won't know about the dragon," said Hubert.

"Maybe you should go and tell her," suggested Benedict.

"Yes, you are right," agreed Hubert. "Mother said that you always know what to do."

History or Mystery?

Learning about history is like being a detective. People who lived a long time ago have left clues about who they were and what they did, but so many clues have been lost, and some of the evidence may not be true. Some of the characters in Hubert's story were real people who lived 800 years ago, some of them were made up characters, and some… well, we are not sure if they were real or not!

The Pied Piper of Hamelin

Hamelin (or Hameln, as it is spelled in Germany) is a town on the river Weser. During the Crusades, this part of Germany was called Saxony. Written in the town chronicles is an account of 130 children being led away by a piper in the year 1284, never to be seen again.

The story was retold by the Brothers Grimm in their collection of 'German Legends', and again by Robert Browning in his poem of 1842. Some people have suggested that the piper was really Nicholas of Cologne, who lured many children away from their homes on the 'Children's Crusade', but although both events are said to have taken place in the 13th century, the dates do not match.

The Children's Crusade

This was reported to have taken place in the year 1212. Two groups of children, one from France and one from Germany set off on a crusade to the Holy Land. Some of the children were captured by pirates and sold as slaves in Egypt.

Their story was told by a priest who said that he also went by ship to Egypt with the children, and it is included in some history books about the Crusades.

Eustace the Monk

Eustace was born in about 1170 and died in about 1217. He is mentioned in the official records from the time of King John. He left the Benedictine order of monks, became an outlaw, and then worked as a pirate in the English Channel.

St Francis of Assisi

Francis was born in 1181 and died in 1226. His mother was a French noblewoman and his father was a silk merchant. Many of the stories about the life of St Francis describe his love for animals and birds. He was also concerned about the cruelty of war and he went to Egypt in 1219 to ask the Sultan to stop the wars of the Crusades.

The Great Pyramid

The pyramid of Khufu is the oldest and largest of the three pyramids at Giza, and it was built over 4,500 years ago. It was 146.6 metres tall when it was first built. It has been worked out that the pyramid was made from about 5.5 million tonnes of limestone, 8,000 tonnes of granite and 500,000 tonnes of mortar.

The Hare

It may seem strange to include the hare in our discussion about history, but finding out about animals and plants and how they live is sometimes called 'Natural History'.

A young hare is called a leveret. It is born with all its fur and its eyes open – unlike a rabbit which is naked and blind at birth. The mother hare is called a doe and she will nurse her leveret for about a month, then it is left to look after itself. Hares rely on their good eyesight, huge ears and keen sense of smell to detect danger. They can run very fast, up to 45 miles per hour, to escape predators, and by changing direction suddenly, they seem to disappear. The behaviour of these timid creatures makes them appear mysterious and magical, and so they have inspired stories and artwork for hundreds of years.